CAJUN NIGHT After CHRISTMAS

CAJUN NIGHT After CHRISTMAS

**Written by Jenny Jackson Moss
and Amy Jackson Dixon**

Illustrated by James Rice

PELICAN PUBLISHING COMPANY
Gretna 2004

First printing, October 2000
Second printing, August 2001
Third printing, September 2004

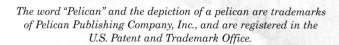

Library of Congress Cataloging-in-Publication Data

Moss, Jackson Jenny
    Cajun night after Christmas / written by Jenny Jackson Moss and Amy Jackson Dixon ; illustrated by
James Rice
        p. cm.
    Summary: In this narrative poem told in Cajun dialect, Pierre the alligator is left behind
in the bayou after helping Santa pull his skiff on Christmas Eve.
    ISBN 1-56554-779-9 (hc : alk. paper)
        1. Santa Claus—Juvenile poetry. 2. Alligators—Juvenile poetry. 3. Christmas—Juvenile
poetry. 4. Cajun—Juvenile poetry. 5. Children's poetry, American. [1. Cajuns—Poetry. 2.
Alligators—Poetry. 3. Narrative poetry. 4. American poetry.] I. Rice, James, 1934- ill. II.
Title.

PS3563.O884578 C35 2000
811'.6—dc21
                                                                            99-085962

Printed in Singapore

Published by Pelican Publishing Company, Inc.
1000 Burmaster Street, Gretna, Louisiana 70053

CAJUN NIGHT AFTER CHRISTMAS

'Twas de night *after* Christmas an' poor ole Boudreau,
His wife she dun spent mo' money den he know.
He lowered hisself into Tante Flo's old chair,
An' his belly popped a button on his long underwear.

De kids were a hollerin' an' a playin' wit' de toys.
Dis cajun, his ears, dey couldn't take no mo' noise.

So Boudreau, he slipped tru de crack in de do'.
He muttered, "Mama, I can't take it no mo'.

"My chirren, dey startin' to drive me so crazy!
I'm hot wit' a fever an' my head's gettin' hazy."

As he ran down de steps, he don't see de stump.
His feet dey did fly an' he fell on his rump!

Den Boudreau he climbed in his two-seated skiff,
To float down de bayou fo' a moonlight drift.
When what to his wanderin' eyes did he spy,
But a not so ordinary alligator pass by.

"Sacre!" he exclaimed, "Dis gator's Pierre!
But it's de night *after* Christmas an' he's floatin' out der.
Manh, I guess dat gator he dun got kinda fat,
An' de skiff couldn't fly wit' a body like dat.

"St. Nicklus, he mus' be right out o' his mind.
He dun' left his good gator, Pierre, behind!"

"Lawsy Mercy, Pierre, jest what will ya do?
Ya sho' don't wanna go float at de zoo!

"Betta call up some prayers an' ax fo' some help.
Before some ole trappa discova yo-self."

So he hitched Pierre's tail to de end of de boat.
An' back down de bayou de pee-row did float.

"Hey Tee-beau, hey Comeaux, Robicheau, an' Yvette.
Stick yo head out de do'. We's got a new pet!
St. Nicklus, his plans mus' have got kinda sour.
He got dat skiff home wit' less gator power."

"Pierre has agreed to come pass a good time."
An' up on de porch dat big gator did climb.
De chirren dey giggled when Pierre went slurp.
He lapped up de water den let out a burp.

So Tee-beau, he did t'ink to pull out de fiddle.
While Mama an' Boudreau put de yams on de griddle.
De laughter, de jokes, de kisses, an' such,
De kids dey jest loved ole Pierre oh so much.

Dey tease him an' poke him an' dress him up funny.
Parade him 'round lookin' fool like a bunny.
Now, Pierre, he be easy, he go wit' de flow.
Loves messin' wit' de chirren, tossin' dem to an' fro.

But, he thought to hisself, *Self, you crazy to stay,*
As a pet at dis house, I gon' run me away!

Den what do pass by but de gator Louise—
She checkin' Pierre an' she like what she sees.

He t'ink, *Manh, she's cute!* Den he ax fo' a date.
She cooked de gumbo, dey danced, an' dey ate.
By de light o' de moon, he confess a' his love.
He know dat dis one, she a' sent from above.

Ain' no time did pass, de two dey did marry.
An' had 'em some kids, so much, manh it's scary.
St. Nick, he stop by 'bout one time a year.
Bring a toy fo' de kids an' have him some cheer.

Pierre an' St. Nick, dey laugh an' dey joke.
'Bout dem good ole days an' 'bout all dere friend-folk.

Den St. Nick, he go off an' shout wit' a glee,
"Pierre, sho' am glad dat it's you an' not me!

"I love dis job, flyin' from town to town.
Well, O-K den, mah friend, I'll see ya around."